for Toby

LITTLE TIGER PRESS LTD,
an imprint of the Little Tiger Group
1 Coda Studios, 189 Munster Road, London SW6 6AW
www.littletiger.co.uk

First published in Great Britain 2005
This edition published 2008

A CIP catalogue record for this book is available from
the British Library

Printed in China • LTP/2700/3594/1020

2 4 6 8 10 9 7 5 3

Hoppity Skip Little Chick

LiTTLE TiGER

LONDON

Jo Brown

Little Chick bounced out of
bed one bright sunny morning.
"Let's play, Mum!" he chirped.

"I need to keep these eggs safe and warm just a little while longer, Little Chick," said Mum, "but I'm sure you'll find someone to play with in the farmyard."

Little Chick tottered
outside and looked around.
Just then some geese rushed past.
 "Honk honk! Follow us!"
they cried.

whiz

ZZZZZ!

Little Chick thought
that running looked fun.
So he ran too!

Little Chick tootled along –
quite fast for a little chick.

whoOooosh!

Faster and faster he ran, so fast his little chick
legs got tangled up and he tripped . . .

yeeeeEEEK!

... and skidded
into a lamb!
"Meeerrrr!" said
the lamb. "That
looks like fun, but
why don't you
try this?"

And she bounced around.

boing!

merrrr!

merrrr!

Little Chick thought
that bouncing looked fun.
So he bounced too!

BOING! Little Chick managed
a little bounce. Well, quite a big
bounce for a little chick.

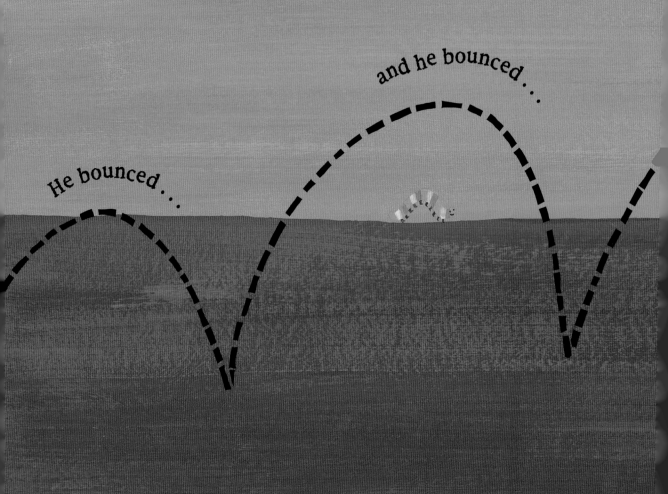

and he bounced...

He bounced...

and he bounced.

He bounced so high that he whizzed through the air . . .

. . . right into a pony!

"Oops!" said the pony. "Nice bouncing, Little Chick,
now why don't you jump over this fence with me?"

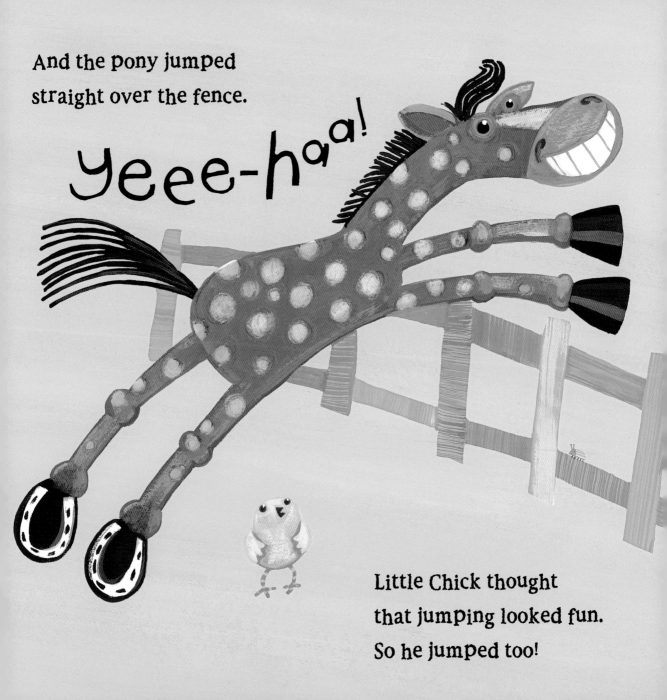

And the pony jumped
straight over the fence.

yeee-haa!

Little Chick thought
that jumping looked fun.
So he jumped too!

Little Chick did a little jump . . . then he did a bigger jump.

Then he did a REALLY
BIG jump, right over the
fence into the next field . . .

Splonggg!

...and landed right
on top of a piglet!

"Oops, sorry!" said Little Chick. "I need more
practice landing, but jumping is great fun!"

Kersplatt!

"If you think that's fun, try this.
It's luuuverly!" said the piglet,
and he rolled around in the mud.

"What fun!"
thought Little Chick.
So he scritched and
he scratched . . .

and then he had a bit
of a roll . . .

and then he did a wiggly
dusty chick dance until there
was dust everywhere.

aaaachooo!

"This is the best
fun of all!" he cried.

"Great rolling, Little Chick!" said the piglet.

"I'm having so much fun today!" said Little Chick.
"All this bouncy-jumpy-roly-running!
I can't wait to tell my mum.
See you later, Piggy!"

And he rushed
across the farmyard
to the hen house . . .

... where he had a HUGE surprise!

"Hello, Little Chick," said Mum.

"Here are your new brothers and sisters."

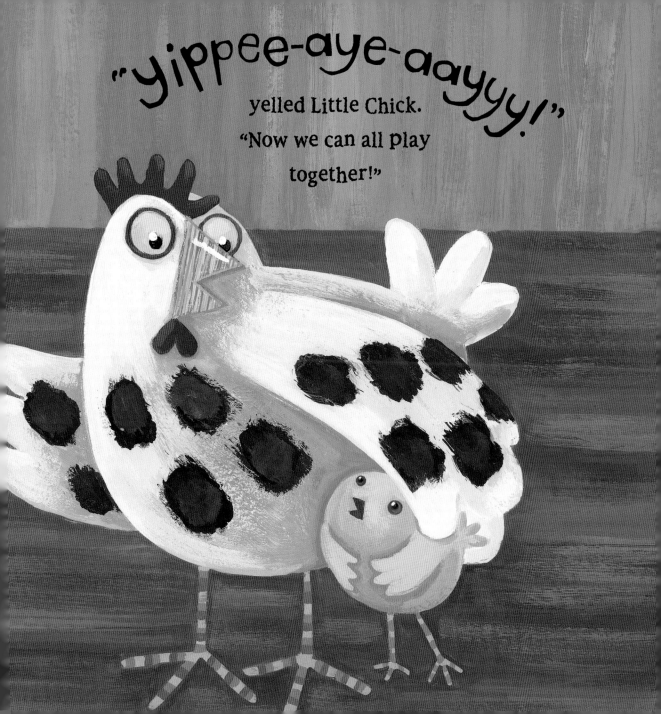

And they played bouncy-jumpy-roly-running
little chick games, all day long! And it
was the greatest fun EVER!

yippeee!